For Malcolm
J.D.
For my little brother James
R.C.

First published 2012 by Macmillan Children's Books
This edition published 2013 by Macmillan Children's Books
a division of Macmillan Publishers Limited
20 New Wharf Road, London N1 9RR
Basingstoke and Oxford
Associated companies throughout the world
www.panmacmillan.com

ISBN: 978-1-4472-2014-5
Text copyright © Julia Donaldson 2012
Illustrations copyright © Rebecca Cobb 2012
Moral rights asserted.

3 5 7 9 8 6 4

A CIP catalogue record for this book is available from the British Library.

Printed in China

Julia Donaldson

THE PAPER DOLLS

Illustrated by
Rebecca Cobb

MACMILLAN CHILDREN'S BOOKS

There was once a girl who
had tiger slippers

and a ceiling with
stars on it

and a butterfly hairslide
which she kept losing

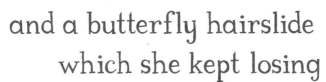

and two goldfish

and a nice mother who helped
her to make some paper dolls.

They were Ticky and Tacky
and Jackie the Backie
and Jim with two noses
and Jo with the bow.

And they danced

and they jumped

and they sang.

And they met a dinosaur
who clawed and roared,
and said, "I'm going to get you!"

But the paper dolls sang,

"You can't get us. Oh no no no!
We're holding hands and we won't let go.
We're Ticky and Tacky and Jackie the Backie
And Jim with two noses and Jo with the bow!"

And they jumped . . .

. . . on to a bus

and rode to a farmyard,
and danced with the pigs.

Then they lay on a rooftop and stared at the stars,
till a tiger slunk out of his den
and he crouched and snarled
and said, "I'll leap up and catch you!"

But the paper dolls sang,

"You can't catch us. Oh no no no!
We're holding hands and we won't let go.

We're Ticky and Tacky and Jackie the Backie
And Jim with two noses and Jo with the bow!"

And they floated . . .

. . . down the stairs

and they danced round
the honey pot

and kicked crumbs
and explored an island

till a fierce crocodile grinned his grin
and gnashed his teeth
and said, "I'm coming to crunch you!"

But the paper dolls laughed, and sang,

"You can't crunch us. Oh no no no!
We're holding hands and we won't let go.

We're Ticky and Tacky and Jackie the Backie
And Jim with two noses and Jo with the bow!"

And they hopped . . .

. . . into the garden

and they sniffed the flowers
and chatted to a ladybird

and lay down in a
forest of grass.

But along came a boy
with a pair of scissors
and he said, "I'll SNIP you!"

And he did.
He snipped them into tiny little pieces
and he said, "You're gone for ever."

But the paper dolls sang,

"We're not gone. Oh no no no!
We're holding hands and we won't let go.
We're Ticky and Tacky and Jackie the Backie
And Jim with two noses and Jo with the bow!"

And the pieces all joined together,
      and the paper dolls flew . . .

... into the little girl's memory
where they found white mice and fireworks,
and a starfish soap,
and a kind granny,
and the butterfly hairslide,
and more and more lovely things each day
and each year.

And the girl grew . . .

. . . into a mother

who helped her own little girl
make some paper dolls.

They were Poppy and Pinkie
and Binky the Blinkie,
and Fred with one eyebrow,
and Flo with the bow.

And they jumped,

and they danced,

and they sang.